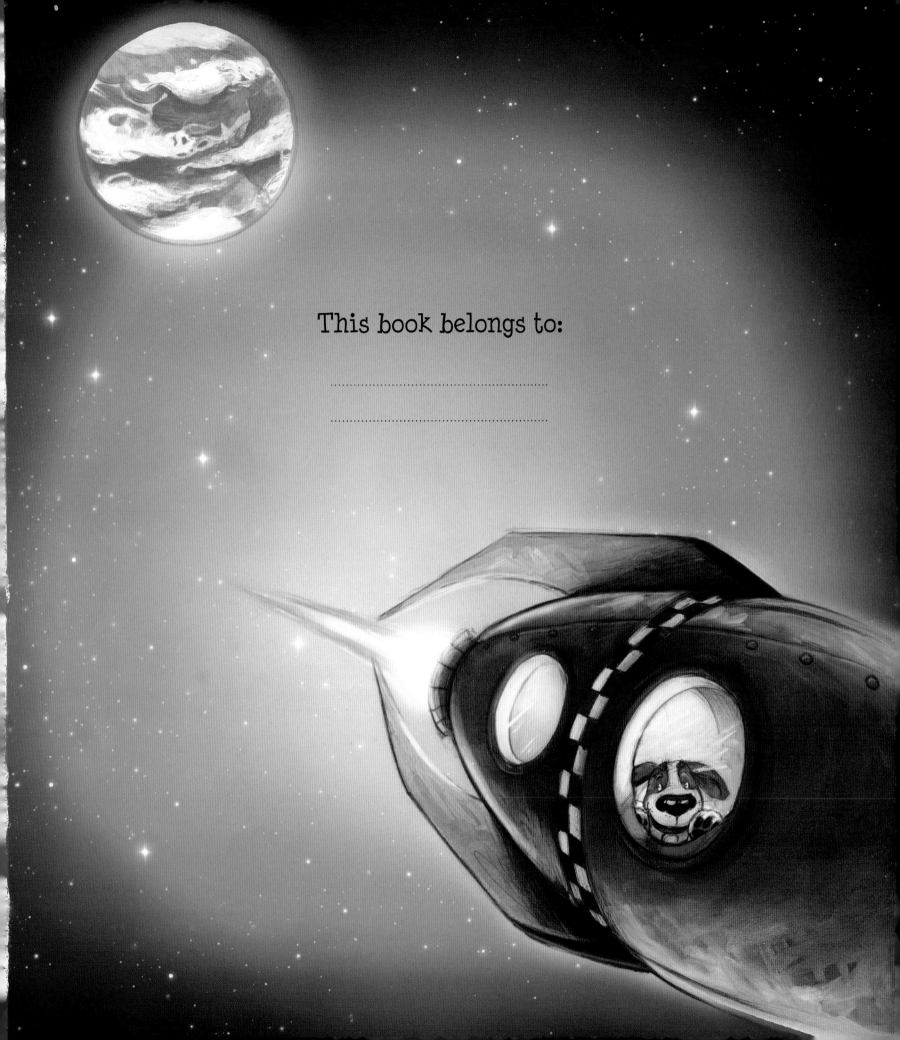

This book belongs to:

....

....

For Fran and Alf - Robert Dunn

Editor: Carly Madden
Designer: Victoria Kimonidou
Editorial Director: Victoria Garrard
Art Director: Laura Roberts-Jensen

First published in the UK in 2015 by QED Publishing
A Quarto Group company, The Old Brewery,
6 Blundell Street, London, N7 9BH

www.qed-publishing.co.uk

A catalogue record for this book is
available from the British Library.

ISBN 978 1 78493 043 1

Printed in China

Space
Walkies

Robert Dunn

QED

QED Publishing

Bailey was Orson's dog,
and Orson was Bailey's boy.

Every day, Bailey loved to sniff
out new adventures.

Adventures like...

...sleeping on Mum's best sheets.

helping himself to Orson's dinner,

or even chewing on
Dad's new slippers!

Bailey's adventures always got him into trouble.

Bailey's favourite adventure
was exploring the
neighbours' gardens.

11

He particularly liked
the garden at number 12,
the one that belonged to
a famous astronaut.

One day, a **gigantic** space rocket was parked on the astronaut's lawn. Nosy Bailey couldn't help but scamper inside to play.

He sniffed at buttons and bounced happily around the control deck.

bounce

bounce

bounce

Then, he accidentally sat on a big red button marked **ignition.**

The engines roared into action, blasting the rocket into Space.

Bailey thought that Orson would be mad at him,
but he was having too much fun to worry.

He didn't know how to fly a rocket,
but luckily it was programmed
to land on the Moon!

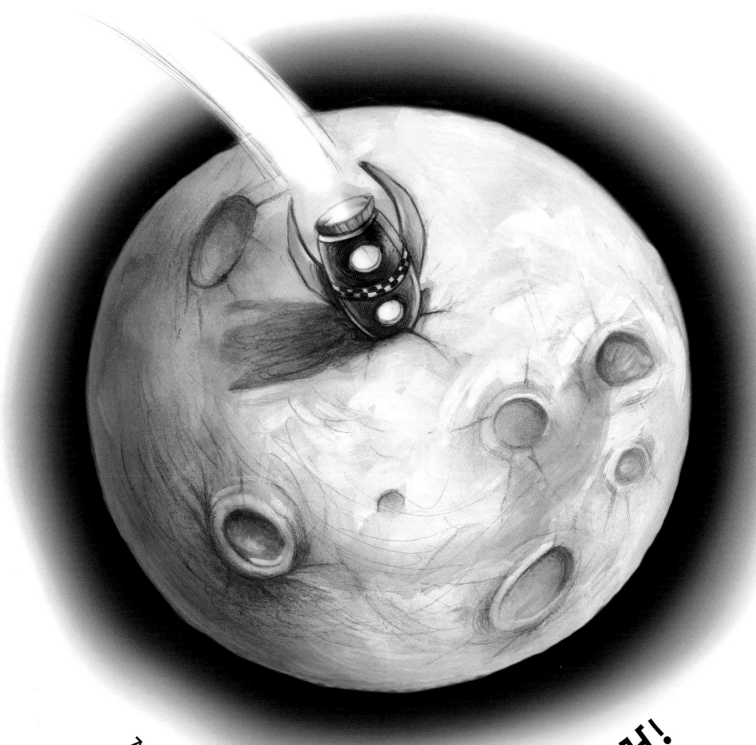

And so it did — with a **FLUMPH!**

Before you could shout,
"Heel, boy!" Bailey was
in his spacesuit and *zooming off*
in search of adventure!

Minutes later, Bailey came shooting back
from the other side of the Moon. He'd found some
new friends to play with – shiny robot pooches
and their equally shiny owner.

"You're a long way from home, aren't you, boy?" beeped the robot owner.

Bailey whined sadly at the thought of home. Orson would normally be walking him in the park about now.

He missed him terribly.

"Don't be sad," said the robot.
"I know what will cheer you up!"

To Bailey's amazement, the robot unscrewed one of his arms and hurled it past him with his other arm.

"Fetch, boy!" he shouted.

Unable to resist fetching the stick-arm, Bailey chased after it as it hurtled through space towards Earth.

Faster and faster went Bailey, tumbling towards Earth at incredible speed.

He eventually caught hold of the
stick-arm and shut his eyes as he prepared
for a frightening crash-landing!

When he opened his eyes however,
he was tucked up in his basket
with Orson at his side.

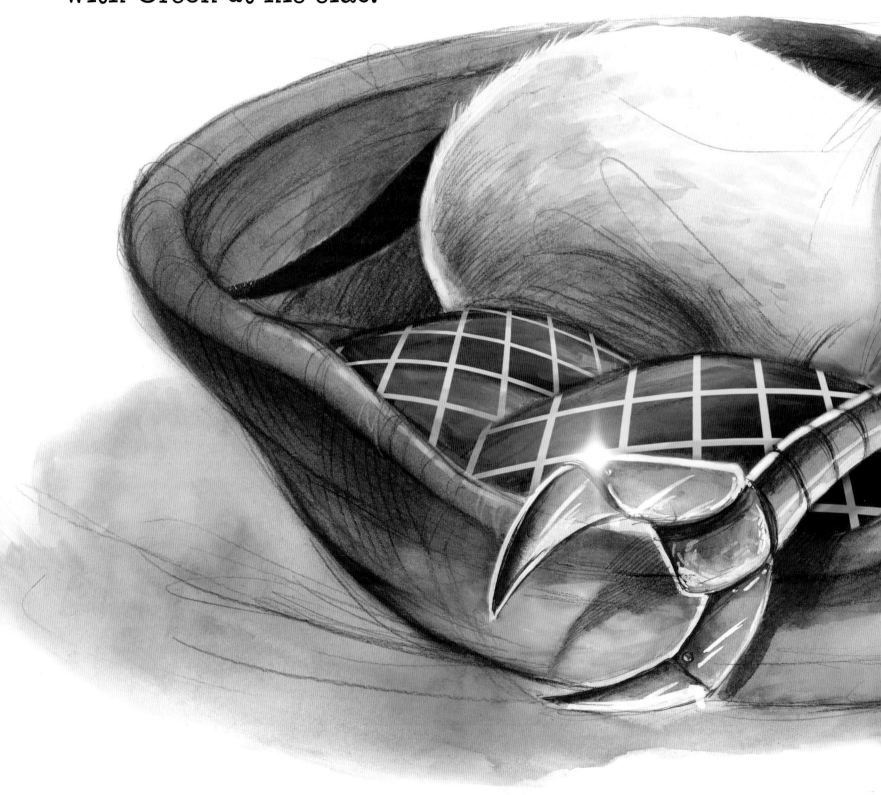

I'll never run away again, he thought, looking up at his friend.

Bailey had dreamt the whole thing! He would be much happier with normal walkies from now on. After all, dogs can't really go on Space walkies, can they?

Next Steps

Show the children the cover again. Could they have guessed what the story is about from looking at the cover?

Bailey is a troublesome but much loved pet. Ask the children if they have any pets. What do they think are the best things about owning a pet? What are the worst things? Which animal would the children most like to have as a pet?

Find out if the children think there might be real aliens in space. Ask the children to draw what they think an alien would look like.

Ask the children to name all of the planets. If it were possible, which one would they most like to visit?

If the children found a new planet what would they call it? What would it look like and who do they think would live there?

While in Space, Bailey felt bad for running off without Orson. Have the children ever really wanted to do something but their parents wouldn't let them? Why do they think their parents made that decision?

Bailey woke up to find that everything was a dream! Do the children believe that his adventure was just a dream? Discuss the children's most memorable dreams.

Can the children think of ideas for Bailey's next adventure? Maybe under the sea in a submarine or deep in the Amazon jungle? What sort of strange characters might Bailey meet on his adventures?